Kappa

Ryunosuke Akutagawa

KAPPA

Translated from the Japanese
by Allison Markin Powell
& Lisa Hofmann-Kuroda

A NEW DIRECTIONS PAPERBOOK ORIGINAL

First published as a New Directions Paperbook Original (NDP1566) in 2023
Manufactured in the United States of America

Library of Congress Control Number: 2023001737

10 9 8 7 6 5 4 3

New Directions Books are published for James Laughlin
by New Directions Publishing Corporation
80 Eighth Avenue, New York 10011

Kappa

Prologue

THIS IS A STORY told by a certain psychiatric patient—
Patient No. 23, to be exact. It is a story he tells to anyone
who will listen. I presume he's at least thirty, though at
first glance he appears quite the youthful-looking mad-
man. He's spent half his life—no, never mind, that's not
important. He relayed the following long-winded story
to me and the hospital director, Dr. S, while sitting stock
still, his knees locked in his arms, and only darting his eyes
toward the window now and again (beyond the barred
window, a single blue oak tree stretched its bare branches
against the wintry sky). However, that's not to say that he
made no gestures at all. Indeed, as he talked on and on, he
became somewhat animated. For example, whenever he
expressed surprise, he'd suddenly throw his head back . . .

I've made every attempt to copy down his story here
just as he told it to me. If, however, the reader is dissatis-
fied with my notes, I suggest they go and pay a visit to
the S. psychiatric ward themselves, which they will find
in XX village, just outside of Tokyo. No doubt they will

3

be greeted by the childlike Patient No. 23, who will bow his head politely as he gestures toward a hard, cushionless chair. Then, with a melancholy smile, he will repeat the following story. At the end of which—oh yes, I remember vividly the expression on his face as he finished speaking—he will leap to his feet and immediately begin shaking his fists in the air, yelling at his listener, "Get out!! Get out, you son of a bitch!!! You're just another stupid, jealous, obscene, shameless, conceited, cruel, selfish animal!! Get out! You son of a bitch!!!"

Chapter 1

IT HAPPENED ONE SUMMER, a few years ago. I had set out with my knapsack, as one does, intending to climb Mount Hotaka from that hot-spring inn at Kamikochi. As you know, there is only one way up Mount Hotaka, which involves following the Azusa River upstream. I'd climbed Mount Hotaka before, of course, not to mention Mount Yari—so as the morning fog descended upon the Azusa valley, I decided to go up without a guide. But that valley in the morning mist—I couldn't get a clear view, the fog refused to lift. In fact, it kept getting heavier and heavier. After walking for about an hour, I considered turning back to the inn. But even if I just headed back to Kamikochi, I'd still need to wait for the fog to lift. Meanwhile, it was only growing thicker by the minute. *Better to keep climbing,* I thought, parting the leaves of the low bamboo grass as I went, so as not to stray too far from the river valley.

For a long time, all I could see was that dense fog surrounding me—although, once in a while, the lush green leaves of a beech tree, suspended from thick branches, or the needles of a fir would emerge from out of the mist. Or sometimes, the face of an ox or a horse would suddenly loom close. But then, they'd disappear into the fog again, just as suddenly as they appeared. Eventually, my feet grew tired, and I began to feel hungry. To make matters worse, my hiking clothes and blanket were soaked through from the moisture in the air, making them extraordinarily heavy. At last, I gave up, and began to make my way back down the river valley, following the sound of running water.

I sat down on a rock near the river's edge and for the time being turned my attention toward food. I got myself situated, opened a can of corned beef, gathered kindling to make a fire—and before I knew it, ten minutes had passed. That fickle fog had ever so slightly begun to clear. As I took a bite of bread, I glanced at my watch. It was already twenty past one! But what shocked me even more than the time was the reflection of a hideous face that appeared for just an instant on my round watch crystal. Startled, I whirled around to look behind me and saw—a kappa! Perched on the rock behind me, just as it looked in pictures. The fact is I'd never seen one of these creatures in real life. It gazed down at me with a look of curiosity, clutching the trunk of a white birch tree with one hand and shading its eyes with the other.

For a moment, I was so shocked I couldn't move. The kappa, too, seemed quite taken aback. Even the hand above its eyes did not budge. Eventually, I sprang to my feet, leaping toward the kappa—but in the same instant, it took off running. Or at least, I think it did. For no sooner had I glimpsed it dodging swiftly away than it disappeared again. More and more flabbergasted, I began searching through the bamboo grass. And suddenly — there it was! Ten feet ahead, it had turned back to look at me, poised to flee again. That in and of itself wasn't particularly strange. Rather, what struck me as odd was the kappa's coloring. At first, standing on that rock and peering down at me, it had been a decidedly gray color. But now, it had gone completely green from head to toe. "Bastard!" I yelled, lunging again toward the kappa. It got away, of course. I must have spent the next half an hour desperately chasing after it, rooting around in the bamboo grass, leaping over rocks.

The kappa was light on its feet, quick as a monkey. I kept losing sight of it as I gave chase frantically, even slipping and falling a few times. But soon, I arrived at the foot of a large horse chestnut tree where, luckily, a grazing ox blocked the kappa's way. The ox had thick horns and bloodshot eyes and the kappa, upon seeing the animal, let out a terrified shriek and somersaulted into a patch of particularly tall grass. "Now I've got him," I muttered to myself as I plunged in after it, close on its heels. But just then, a gaping hole I hadn't noticed before opened up beneath me. The instant my fingertips touched the kappa's slippery back, I tumbled headfirst into deep darkness. As I was falling, I suddenly remembered there had been a "Kappa Bridge" near the old Kamikochi inn — the human mind comes up with the most preposterous things in life-or-death situations — and then, what happened after that, I can't remember except for a brilliant light that flashed before my eyes. And before I knew it, I lost consciousness.

Chapter 2

SOMETIME LATER, WHEN I finally came to, I found myself lying faceup surrounded by a crowd of Kappas. Not only that, one of the Kappas, a pince-nez perched on his thick bill, was kneeling beside me and holding a stethoscope to my chest. When he saw that I had opened my eyes, he gestured to me to remain calm, and then called out to one of the Kappas behind him, "*Quax quax*." Whereupon two Kappas appeared, carrying a stretcher. Without any fuss, I was put on this stretcher and quietly carried through the crowd of Kappas, off along a broad avenue. The cityscape that passed on either side of me looked exactly like Ginza-dori, one of the main boulevards in Tokyo. There was an array of shop awnings shaded by a row of zelkova trees, and another row of trees sandwiched a roadway, with cars speeding down it.

Just as I thought we were turning onto a narrow side street, I was carried inside a house. As I would subsequently learn, it was the home of that pince-nez-wearing Kappa, a doctor called Chac. Chac put me onto a quaint and tidy bed. Then he had me drink a glass of clear liquid, some kind of medicine. As I lay on the bed, I was at Chac's mercy. Indeed, my joints ached so much that it was impossible for me to move.

From then on, Chac came to examine me two or three times a day without fail. About every third day, the Kappa I had first caught sight of—a fisherman called Bagg—came to visit. Kappas know far more about us humans than we know about them. This must be because Kappas have captured us humans much more often than we have captured them. Maybe "capturing" isn't quite the right word, but prior to my arrival a number of humans had visited Kappa Land, and many had ended up spending their whole lives here. And the reason why is, not being Kappas, we have the privilege of getting by without working, simply because we're humans. In fact, Bagg told me about a young road laborer or some such who, after happening to come to this land, took a female Kappa as his wife and lived here for the rest of his life. However, this female Kappa was apparently quite skilled at cheating on her road-laborer husband, since she was also the most beautiful Kappa in all the land.

After about a week, as required by the law of this land, I was designated a "resident under special protection" and moved next door to Chac. Despite how small my home was, it was quite elegantly appointed. Of course, Kappa Land's civilization is not much different from ours—at least not from Japanese civilization. The drawing room faced out onto the street, with a small piano in the corner and framed etchings hanging on the walls. The only quibble I had with the house was that the table and chairs were designed for Kappas, and thus, size-wise, were more fit for a child's room.

This was where, every evening around sundown, I would receive Chac and Bagg for lessons in the Kappa language. They weren't my only visitors, of course. Being a resident under special protection, I was quite the curiosity. Another Kappa called Geyl, who presided over a glass company, used to come around quite frequently as well. He was often accompanied by Chac, who'd always check my blood pressure. During those first couple of weeks, though, the one I became friendliest with was that fisherman called Bagg.

One warm and muggy evening, I was sitting across the table from Bagg the fisherman. Then, I don't know what Bagg was thinking, but he suddenly fell silent while staring at me intently, his big eyes even bigger than usual. Of course, I thought this was strange, so I said, "*Quax,* Bagg, *quo quel quan*?" Translated into Japanese, this meant, "Hey, Bagg, what's the matter?" But Bagg didn't answer. Instead, he stood up suddenly, then started wagging his tongue and leaping about, hopping around like a frog and making a scene. I got more and more unnerved, and I quietly stood up from my chair and made a beeline for the door. Just then, luckily, who should appear but Dr. Chac.

"Hey, Bagg, what are you doing?" Chac demanded, glaring at Bagg over his pince-nez: "Cut it out!"

Bagg looked contrite and began apologizing to Chac,

touching his head repeatedly. "I'm terribly sorry. Honestly, I just thought it would be fun to play a prank on him and got carried away. Please, sir, I ask for your forgiveness, too."

Chapter 3

BU T BEFORE I GO ON, I need to explain a thing or two about Kappas. Apparently there is still considerable debate over whether or not these creatures actually exist. But, having myself spent time living among them, I can tell you that there is absolutely no reason to doubt their existence. What do they look like, you might ask? Their heads are covered with short hairs, and they have webbed feet and hands. They look remarkably similar to the illustrations that appear in Koga Toan's historical investigation, *An Inquiry into the Water Tiger*. They are about three feet tall, give or take. According to Dr. Chac, they usually weigh anywhere from twenty to thirty pounds—although once in a while you might see one that weighs as much as fifty pounds. They also have an oval-shaped plate on top of their head, and this plate, it seems, grows harder as the Kappa ages. For example, Bagg is quite a bit older than Chac, so his plate has a completely different texture.

But perhaps the strangest thing about Kappas is the color of their skin. Unlike humans, Kappas do not have a fixed skin color. Instead, they change color according to their environment. For example, a Kappa's skin will turn green when they're in the grass and gray when they're on top of a rock. Of course, this ability to camouflage themselves is not unique to Kappas—chameleons do it too. And it may be that Kappas are not so different from chameleons, at least as far as their skin tissue is concerned. When I discovered this particular characteristic of Kappas, I suddenly remembered something I had read in a book of folklore, which said that Kappas in the western part of Japan tend to be green, while those in the northeast area tend to be red. That memory called to mind the moment, as I was chasing Bagg, when suddenly he was no longer visible. Kappas also seem to have a thick layer of fat beneath their skin. This is why, despite living in an underground country, whose climate is quite cool (the average temperature is said to be around 50 degrees Fahrenheit) you will never see a Kappa wearing clothes. And while most Kappa carry a number of objects on their person—spectacles, a tobacco box, a coin purse, to name a few—they aren't at all inconvenienced, because they have a small pouch on their stomach, somewhat like a kangaroo's, for stowing their things. I was amused by the fact that Kappas don't cover up any part of their body, not even their midsection. Once, I asked Bagg why not. To which he replied, doubling over with raucous laughter: "It's funny to me that you *do* cover it up!"

Chapter 4

GRADUALLY I BEGAN to understand the words that Kappas use in their everyday speech, and so began to get the hang of their manners and customs. The strangest among these was that they find amusing the things that humans take seriously, while at the same time, they take seriously things that we are amused by—it's quite bizarre. For example, we take things like Justice and Humanity seriously, but when Kappas hear of this, they can't help laughing. In other words, the standards for what is comical to Kappas and what is comical to us are completely different. One time, I was having a conversation with Dr. Chac about birth control. Chac burst out laughing, his mouth wide open, so much so that his pince-nez fell off. I got angry, of course, and demanded to know what was so funny. This is roughly what I remember as his answer, though I may very well be mistaken about some fine points (at that time I didn't yet fully understand the language):

"But thinking only about what suits the parents is what's so odd. Isn't that rather self-centered?"

And moreover, from the human perspective, there is nothing so odd as the way Kappas give birth. In fact, not long after this, I visited Bagg's hut just as his wife was about to have a baby. Childbirth for Kappas is somewhat the same as for us, in that they have a doctor or a midwife to help. However, when it comes time to give birth, the father puts his mouth to the mother's genitals and—as if he were speaking into a telephone—he shouts the question, "Give some thought as to whether you're going to be born into this world or not, and get back to us!" Bagg did this very thing, kneeling before his wife, and repeating it several times. Then he gargled with some antiseptic medicine that was on the table. It seemed that the child inside his wife's belly was feeling a bit hesitant, given the reply that came in a small voice:

"I do not wish to be born. The hereditary mental illness of my father is bad enough—and besides, I believe that life as a Kappa is a poor existence."

Hearing this, Bagg scratched his head awkwardly. But the midwife immediately thrust a thick glass tube into his wife's genitals and injected some kind of liquid. His wife let out a heavy sigh of relief. At once, her until now huge belly deflated, collapsing like a hot-air balloon when the air is let out.

Of course, as you might gather from such a response, no sooner are Kappa children born than they are already walking and talking. I heard from Chac that there was a child who gave a lecture on the existence of G-d just twenty-six days after he was born. (That child did end up dying in his second month, however.)

While we're on the subject of childbirth, I may as well mention the large poster I happened to see on a street corner, in my third month there. The bottom of the poster featured drawings of twelve or thirteen Kappas, playing trumpets and wielding swords and the like. Then, above those, there was the spiral lettering that Kappas use, which looks just like the springs of a clock. Here's basically what it said, if I were to translate that spiral lettering (and, again, my version may be a little off, though Rapp, the student I happened to be with, read the words out loud for me and these are the notes I took down):

RECRUITING FOR THE GENETIC VOLUNTEER CORPS!!!

WANTED: MALE AND FEMALE KAPPAS IN GOOD HEALTH!!!

ERADICATE BAD GENES: MARRY AN UNHEALTHY KAPPA!!!

Of course, I told Rapp right then and there what I found objectionable about this kind of thing. But Rapp—and not only him but all the Kappas who were near the poster—roared with laughter.

"Objectionable? But from everything you've told us, you humans do the exact same thing. Why do you think your sons fall for the housemaids, and your daughters fall for the chauffeurs? That's everyone unconsciously eradicating bad genes. Besides, compared to the volunteer corps that you were talking about the other day—killing each other over a single railroad—it seems to me that our volunteers are far more refined."

Rapp said this with a straight face, though as he spoke, his belly fat rippled in amusement. But there was no time to laugh—while I had been speaking with Rapp, one of the other Kappas had taken advantage of my inattention and stolen my fountain pen. I lunged after him, but his sleek Kappa skin made him hard to catch. No sooner had I grasped him than he got away, his wiry, mosquito-like body shooting off at such a speed, as if he'd been catapulted.

Chapter 5

I'M GRATEFUL TO RAPP, as much as I am to Bagg, for all that he did to help me. But the one thing I'll never forget is when he introduced me to a Kappa named Tok. Tok was the poet among their friends. He had long hair, making him no different from the poets you'd find among us. Sometimes, when I was bored, I'd go over to Tok's house to kill time. There, inside his cramped room lined with potted alpine plants, I'd find him writing poems, smoking, and living his best, carefree life. In one corner of the room, there would be a female Kappa, knitting or doing something or other (Tok was a polyamorist, so he didn't have what we'd refer to as a wife). When Tok saw me, he would always smile (however, I should note that a Kappa's smile is not such a good thing, or at least, in the beginning I thought their smiles were quite creepy) and say—

"Ah, so good of you to come! Pull up a chair."

Tok would often talk about the Kappa lifestyle, Kappa art, and so forth. As far as he was concerned, there was nothing so ridiculous as the life of an ordinary Kappa.

Parents and children, husbands and wives, brothers and sisters — their sole pleasure seemed to be making each other altogether miserable. Above all, he believed that this thing called "the family" was just beyond stupid. One time, Tok pointed toward the window and nearly spat out, "Would you just look at that foolishness?" There was a young Kappa staggering along the road, gasping for air as he walked with seven or eight Kappas hanging all over him, two of whom appeared to be his parents. For my part, I was impressed by the self-sacrificing spirit of this young Kappa, and lauded his courageousness.

"Hmm, you have all the qualifications to become a citizen of this country, too ... By the way, do you happen to be a socialist?"

Naturally, I responded *qua* (in the Kappa language, this means "affirmative").

"So you're telling me you'd sacrifice one genius for the sake of a hundred ordinary people?"

"Well, what are you, then? Someone told me you're an anarchist ..."

"Me? I'm an Übermensch," Tok declared proudly. (Well, a direct translation would be more like Überkappa.)

This Tok also held some peculiar ideas about art. According to him, art should exist for art's sake and nothing else — thus, by extension, artists must also be Übermenschen, going beyond notions of good and evil. Then again, Tok wasn't the only Kappa who held this opinion. Tok's friends, also Kappa poets, seemed to share a similar outlook.

Sometimes I went with Tok to hang out at the Übermensch Club. Among those who gathered there were poets, novelists, playwrights, critics, painters, musicians, and sculptors—all of them amateurs, of course, but Übermenschen nonetheless. They would gather under the bright lights of the salon, chatting in a lively manner. What's more, they would sometimes show off their über-menschness to one another. For example, one time a male sculptor grabbed a young Kappa, took him between the large potted holly ferns, and began vigorously making love to him. Another time, a female novelist climbed on top of a table, drank sixty bottles of absinthe, then promptly collapsed, rolled under the table, and died.

One moonlit night, I was walking home from one of these Übermensch gatherings, arm in arm with Tok. He was unusually quiet. Soon, we passed by a small window, through which we could see faint shadows flickering in the firelight. Inside, there was a family of Kappas sitting around the dinner table—what appeared to be a husband and wife, and their three Kappa children. Letting out a little sigh, Tok suddenly turned to me and said:

"I think of myself as a polyamorist Übermensch, but whenever I see a family like that, I can't help but feel a little envious."

"Don't you think that's a bit of a contradiction?"

But Tok just stood there under the moonlight, arms crossed, gazing through the window at the peaceful scene of the Kappas sitting around the dinner table. After a while, he said:

"You know, I suppose even those eggs right there are more health-giving than love."

Chapter 6

ACTUALLY, KAPPA LOVE is quite a bit different from human love. As soon as a female Kappa happens upon a male Kappa she thinks is "the one," she will chase after him with reckless abandon. In fact, I myself once witnessed a female madly pursuing a male. And that's not the half of it! The young Kappa, why, her entire family—parents and siblings as well—all banded together in pursuit. The Kappa male is really a miserable creature. Even if he's lucky enough to avoid being caught, he often ends up bedridden for a good two or three months after all that running around. One time, I was at home reading Tok's poetry collection when Rapp the student came rushing to my front door. He tumbled into the house and collapsed on the floor, saying breathlessly, "I'm in trouble! She's finally glommed on to me!"

I immediately tossed aside the poetry book and bolted the door. But when I peered through the keyhole, all I saw was a female Kappa, quite petite in stature and with a thick layer of white sulfur powder on her face, pacing back and forth outside the door. From that day on, Rapp slept at my place for several weeks. At one point his bill rotted away and fell off entirely.

However it's not necessarily unheard of for Kappa males to pursue Kappa females in earnest. But when this does happen, it's usually because the Kappa female has acted in a way that makes chasing her irresistible. Once, for example, I saw a Kappa male driven quite mad by the chase. The female Kappa would purposely pause midflight to look back at him and present herself on all fours. To top it off, she waited until just the right moment to allow herself to be caught, while appearing truly crestfallen. I watched as the male Kappa lay there on the ground for a spell, still holding the female Kappa. But when he finally got up, he wore a pitiful expression—whether from frustration or regret—I really cannot describe it. Though that's nothing compared to this: another time I saw a small Kappa male chasing a Kappa female. As per usual, the Kappa female was fleeing in her seductive way. When all of a sudden, a large Kappa male came walking over from the other side of the street, snorting as he went. As soon as she saw him, the Kappa female suddenly let out a piercing scream. "HELP! Somebody help me! That Kappa is trying to kill me!" Without missing a beat, the big male Kappa grabbed the small one and held him down in the middle of the busy street. His webbed hands grasped at the air a few times and then he expired right there. The female Kappa clung to the big male's neck and grinned.

Every single one of the male Kappas I knew said—as if they had agreed upon it in advance—that they had been pursued by a female. Not even Bagg, who was married with children, was exempt. In fact, he'd been caught two or three times. Only the philosopher called Magg (he was the Kappa who lived next door to the poet Tok) had never been caught. This may have been because Magg was a rather unattractive Kappa, but it also could have been attributed to the fact that he hardly ever set foot out of the house. Sometimes I would go over to Magg's place to have a chat. He always had an iridescent stained-glass lantern lit, and I would find him sitting at his long-legged desk, reading a thick book. One time, Magg and I got into a discussion about love among Kappas.

"Why doesn't the government have stricter regulations about females chasing after males?"

"Well, one reason is because so few government officials are female. And female Kappas are much more jealous than male Kappas. If only there were more female officials, then surely male Kappas could live their lives without being chased as they are now. But I'm not sure that would be a very effective solution. What I mean is, the female officials would just chase after the male Kappas."

"So you're saying that your way is the path to happiness?"

In response, Magg got up from his chair, took my hands in his, and sighed. "You are not one of us Kappas. So of course you wouldn't understand. But there are times when even I experience the desire to be pursued by one of those awful females."

Chapter 7

SOMETIMES I'D GO OUT to concerts with Tok. To this day, I will never forget the third concert we ever went to. The concert hall wasn't too different from what you'd find in Japan. It had stadium seating, in which three or four hundred male and female Kappas sat together, each holding a copy of the program as they listened intently to the performance. At this third concert, I was sitting in the front row with Tok and his female companion, along with Magg the philosopher. Just as the cello solo ended, a Kappa with unusually small eyes ascended the stage, casually carrying a musical score. According to the program, he was a famous composer named Craback. Just as the program stated ... but in fact, there was no need to look at the program—since Craback was a member of the Übermensch club that Tok belonged to, I recognized him right away.

"Klavierstück—Craback" (the programs in this country, as in ours, usually included a lot of German words).

After a burst of applause Craback gave a small bow in

our direction and calmly approached the piano. And then, maintaining his casual demeanor, he began to play a piece he had composed himself. According to Tok, Craback's genius was unparalleled by any other musicians this country had produced. I was intrigued by Craback's music, of course, as well as his lyric poetry, which was one of my interests, so I listened with rapture to the sounds emanating from the grand piano. Both Tok and Magg seemed even more captivated than me. Only the pretty (well, at least according to what the Kappas said) female Kappa remained in full possession of herself. From time to time she would flick out her long tongue in annoyance as she sat clutching the program. According to Magg, around ten years ago, she had unsuccessfully pursued Craback, and held a grudge against the musician to this day.

Playing with great passion, Craback threw his whole body into the music, striking the piano keys as though in heated combat. Then, suddenly, a voice reverberated like thunder throughout the hall: "PERFORMANCE VERBOTEN!" Startled by the voice, I reflexively whirled around to look behind me. The voice unmistakably belonged to a distinguished-looking police officer who was sitting in the very last row. When I turned to look at him, this police officer, still lounging in his seat, again yelled, and this time more loudly: "PERFORMANCE VERBOTEN!" And then—

And then, all hell broke loose. "POLICE TYRANNY!" "Play on, Craback, play on!" "Stupid!" "Bastard!" "Fall back!" "Don't give in!" In the midst of this uproar of voices, chairs toppled, programs flew, and as if that weren't enough (I don't know who actually threw them), an empty bottle of cider, some pebbles, and even a half-eaten cucumber rained down on us. Completely dumb-founded, I tried to ask Tok what in the world was happening. But Tok was no help—he was standing on top of his chair, shouting "Play on, Craback! Play on!" Anyway, I guess Tok's female companion had by this time forgotten all about her animosity toward Craback because she, too, just like Tok, was shouting "POLICE TYRANNY!" Not knowing what else to do, I turned to Magg, and asked: "What's going on?"

"Oh, this? This kind of thing happens quite often here. When it comes to painting and literature and that sort of thing..."

Magg would duck his head a little every time an object flew past, but otherwise remained calm as he explained things to me.

"When it comes to paintings and literature, their meaning is obvious, so there are no prohibitions on selling or exhibiting works like that. There are, however, bans on performances. When it comes down to it, no matter how much a piece of music may corrupt public morals, a Kappa would never know it, not having ears to hear it."

"And that police officer does?"

"That's a good question. Maybe as he was listening to the melody, it reminded him of the way his heart pounds when he makes love to his wife, or something like that."

Meanwhile, the uproar had grown even more intense. Craback, still facing the piano, cast a defiant look back toward us. Yet however hard he tried to remain above it all, on the stage there was no avoiding the various items that flew at him. As a result, every two or three seconds he'd have to adjust his carefully assumed posture. But all in all, he managed to maintain a sense of dignity befitting a great musician, his small eyes glittering fiercely all the while.

And I—I, too, of course, tried to protect myself from harm by using Tok as a shield. But in the end, my sense of curiosity got the better of me, and I continued questioning Magg in earnest.

"But don't you find such censorship unreasonable?"

"What? Compared to the censorship exercised everywhere else, we are far more progressive. Take Japan, for example. Why, only a month ago—"

But unfortunately, just as he was saying this, an empty bottle hit Magg square in the head, and with a single "*quack*" (this being a form of interjection) he lost consciousness.

Chapter 8

I HAD TAKEN a strange liking to Geyl, who ran a glass company. He was a capitalist among capitalists. I doubt that any Kappa in Kappa Land had a belly as big as Geyl's. And when he sat in his easy chair, Geyl was the picture of happiness—with his wife who looked like a peeled lychee and his kid who resembled a cucumber on either side of him. Sometimes Dr. Chac and a judge named Pepp would bring me over to Geyl's house for supper. Also, thanks to a letter of introduction from Geyl, I was able to tour the many different factories that he and his friends had connections with. Among these, the one I found especially interesting was the book manufacturer's factory. I went there with a young Kappa engineer, and when I saw the huge hydroelectrically powered machines, I had to admire the industrial advancement of Kappa Land. As I understood it, in one year, they produced seven million books. What surprised me was not the number of books, but rather, with what little effort they printed so many. You see, here in Kappa Land, all you needed to do was funnel raw materials—paper, ink, and gray powder—into a huge machine, and within a matter of minutes, out came countless books of all shapes and sizes: A1, B1, even half-A1 format. As I watched this cascade of book after book, I turned to the proud engineer and asked what that gray powder was. To which he responded, still standing before the gleaming apparatus, "Oh, that?" He sounded almost bored by my question. "It's donkey brains. Once it's dried, it's ground into powder. The going rate is about two or three sen per ton."

Of course, this sort of industrial miracle occurs in Kappa factories manufacturing paintings and music as well. In fact, according to Geyl, there are, on average, seven or eight hundred kinds of new contraptions invented per month, so that goods can be mass-produced without even hiring a labor force. Consequently, he said, no less than forty or fifty thousand factory workers have been laid off. And yet, despite reading the newspaper every morning when I was there, I never seen the word "strike" mentioned even once. I found it odd, so one time when I had been invited to Geyl's for supper with Pepp and Chac, I took the opportunity to inquire why this was so.

"Well, that's because we eat 'em," Geyl said nonchalantly between puffs of his after-dinner cigar. But I didn't know what he meant by "eat 'em." Chac, wearing his pince-nez, sensed my incomprehension and cut in to offer an explanation:

"Those factory workers were all killed and made into food. Here, look at this newspaper. Just this month, 44,764 laborers were dismissed, so the price of meat has gone down accordingly."

"The factory workers just submit to being killed, without a word of protest?"

"Even if they kicked up a fuss, it still wouldn't matter. The Workers' Slaughter Rule is the law," Pepp added, scowling from behind a potted bayberry plant.

Naturally this left me feeling a bit uneasy. But our host Geyl, along with Pepp and Chac, seemed to find it perfectly reasonable. In fact, Chac even seemed to mock me, saying with a laugh: "It saves workers the trouble of committing suicide or starving to death. Think of it as a state-sponsored shortcut! They just give them a little toxic gas, it doesn't hurt a bit."

"But then you . . . eat their flesh?"

"Don't kid yourself. If you were to ask Magg, he'd laugh in your face. What about in your country—don't you make the daughters of the proletariat into prostitutes? So your outrage about eating workers' flesh is just sentimentalism."

Geyl, who had been listening in on this exchange, offered me the plate of sandwiches that was on the table near him, saying cooly, "Well, what do you think? Would you like to try some? They're workers' flesh."

Instinctively I flinched. No, more than that. I raced out of Geyl's drawing room, leaving behind the laughing voices of Pepp and Chac. It was a stormy night, and I couldn't see any stars above the houses. As I rushed back to my own house in the darkness, I couldn't stop vomiting. My bile spewed out, gleaming palely even in the night shadows.

Chapter 9

GEYL THE GLASS COMPANY PRESIDENT was a downright amiable Kappa. Sometimes I'd go out with him to the club he belonged to, and have a great time. This was in part because I felt much more at ease at Geyl's club than at Tok's Übermensch Club. And despite the fact that conversations with Geyl did not have the same level of depth as those I had with Magg the philosopher, he showed me an entirely new world. He'd always speak cheerfully on a number of topics as he stirred the coffee in his cup with a spoon made of solid gold.

Anyway, one foggy night, I was talking with Geyl, a vase of winter roses between us on the table. If I remember correctly, the room was in the Viennese Secession style, which of course meant that everything, including the tables and chairs, was white with gold trim. Geyl was grinning smugly from ear to ear—even more so than usual—as he talked about the Quorax Party that had just taken power. "Quorax" is a meaningless word that basically amounts to an exclamation, so I'd probably translate it as something like "Well, well!" But in any case, the Quorax were the political party advocating for "the interests of all Kappas."

"The head of the Quorax party is a well-known politician named Roppe. Bismarck is known for the saying, 'Honesty is the best diplomacy,' but Roppe uses honesty even in domestic politics—"

"But Roppe's speeches ..."

"I'm telling you, every speech is a complete lie. But everyone knows that, so in the end, it might as well be the truth. It is simply due to the prejudices of your own kind that you perceive it as a lie. We Kappas, unlike you—ugh, never mind. What I actually want to talk about is Roppe. Now, Roppe controls the Quorax party, but there's someone else who controls Roppe, and that is Kuikui, the editor of the Pou-Fou newspaper." (This word, "Pou-Fou," is also a completely meaningless interjection. If hard-pressed to translate it, I'd have to go for something like "Ahh.") "But don't think for a minute that Kuikui is his own boss. No—the one who controls Kuikui is sitting right here in front of you."

"But—this might come across as a bit rude, but doesn't the Pou-Fou newspaper generally take the side of the workers? The fact that the editor defers to you strikes me as a bit—"

"The *journalists* at the Pou-Fou take the side of the workers, of course," said Geyl. "But who do you think controls them? Kuikui! And Kuikui has no choice but to accept my backing," he said, toying with his solid gold spoon, his smile as sly as ever.

Observing Geyl in moments like these made me . . . not hate him exactly, but I couldn't help sympathizing with the journalists.

Geyl seemed to intuit the meaning of my silence right away. "Look, not all of the Pou-Fou journalists support the workers," he said, puffing out his belly. "You must understand that we Kappa are loyal to no one but ourselves . . . Besides, what's even more troublesome is that I, Geyl, am being controlled by yet another. And who do you suppose that is? My wife! The beautiful Mrs. Geyl." He gave a hearty laugh.

"If anything, that sounds like a good thing," I said.

"Oh yes, I'm quite happy about it. But I only say that to you because you're not a Kappa, so I can speak my mind in front of you."

"So basically, Mrs. Geyl controls the Quorax Party."

"Yes, we do get that sort of thing once in a while . . . And I'll be damned if the war that broke out seven years ago didn't start because of a Kappa female."

"War? So this country had a war, too?"

"Oh yes. And perhaps in the future there will be more, we just don't know when. As long as there are neighboring countries . . ."

And this is when I first learned that Kappa Land was not an isolationist country, politically speaking. Theoretically, Kappas regarded otters as their enemy—at least, according to Geyl's explanation. But the otters were competitively equipped, militarily speaking.

I was considerably interested in this story about the war between the Kappas and the otters. (In any case, that

Kappas had a formidable enemy in the otters was a fact unknown even to the author of *Inquiry into the Water Tiger*, or to Yanagita Kunio, who wrote *Legends of the Mountainous Islands*.)

"Of course, even before the war began, both countries were eyeing each other suspiciously, locked in a stalemate. That's because we feared each other. Then, an otter who happened to be in this country went to visit a Kappa couple. The female Kappa was planning to kill her husband—who, to be fair, was a libertine—though we can't discount as a potential motive the fact that she was on his life insurance ..."

"And did you know the couple?"

"Yes—well, at least the husband. My wife says terrible things about him. But I don't think he's a bad guy, if you ask me. Just a lunatic who was severely paranoid about his wife catching him ... anyway, the female Kappa put potassium cyanide in her husband's cocoa, but she accidentally handed it to her guest, the otter. So of course, the otter died. Then—"

"Then you went to war?"

"Well yes, unfortunately, because that otter was a decorated hero."

"And who ended up winning the war?"

"We did, of course. Though 369,500 Kappas admirably laid down their lives for the cause. But that's nothing compared to what the enemy lost. Whatever furs we have in Kappa Land are mostly otter pelts. My contribution to the war effort, aside from manufacturing glass, was shipping coal cinders to the battlefield."

"What were the coal cinders used for?"

"They were used as provisions, what else? If we get hungry enough, Kappas will eat anything."

"Please don't get angry at me for asking, but … coal cinders? For the Kappas on the front lines? That would be a scandal in our country."

"It was a scandal here too. But as long as I admit as much, no one makes a fuss. As Magg the philosopher always says: 'Confess thy faults: and they shall be expunged.' But in addition to profit, I was motivated by fierce patriotism."

Just at that moment, a server from the club came in and bowed to Geyl.

"Excuse me sir, but a fire has broken out in the house next door to yours," he said, as though making a proclamation.

"F—ff—fire?!" Geyl leapt to his feet in surprise. Naturally, I followed suit.

"However, it has already been put out," the waiter added, remaining perfectly calm.

Geyl seemed to be smiling through his tears as he walked the server to the door. Though at times I had hated this glass company president, as I regarded the expression on his face at that moment, he suddenly became a perfectly ordinary Kappa to me—not a capitalist or any such thing. I plucked a single flower from a vase of winter roses and handed it to him:

"Even if the fire was put out, I'm sure your wife is in shock. Here, bring her this."

"Thank you," Geyl said as he grasped my hands. Then he suddenly broke out into a grin.

"The house next door is a rental property of mine. So at least I'll be able to collect insurance money on it," he said in a low voice.

Geyl's smile at that moment—I could neither hate it nor disparage it. Though I remember it vividly to this very day.

Chapter 10

"WHAT'S WRONG? ARE you still feeling down?" I asked Rapp the student.

It was the day after the fire. He was sitting in a chair in my drawing room while I smoked a cigarette. In point of fact, Rapp was sitting with his left leg propped on his right one, staring absently down at the floor in a way that hid his rotten bill.

"Come on, Rapp, tell me what's bothering you."

"Oh, well, it's nothing really."

When at last Rapp raised his head, he spoke in a sad, nasal voice.

"Today, as I was looking out the window," he went on, "I casually remarked, 'Hey, the carnivorous violets have bloomed,' when all of a sudden my younger sister went pale and—would you believe it—she snapped at me, 'So now I'm a carnivorous violet?' And then, to make matters worse, my mom began to lash out at me too—she always takes my sister's side."

"Why would your sister find it offensive for you to say that the carnivorous violets had bloomed?"

"Well, I guess she probably thought it was a reference to her catching a male Kappa. Anyway, that's when my aunt—the one who doesn't get along with my mum—jumped in. And then things really went to hell. What's more, my dad—perpetual drunk that he is—overheard the argument and started whaling on any and all of us. And while all that was going on, my younger brother saw it as an opportunity to steal my mom's wallet and take himself straight to the cinema to see some movie. I swear … I've really …"

Rapp buried his face in his hands and, without another word, burst into tears. Naturally I felt sorry for him. But, at the same time, I couldn't help but be reminded of the poet Tok's contempt for the family system. I patted Rapp on the shoulder and did my best to console him.

"Ah, this kind of thing happens everywhere. You've got to buck up your courage!"

"But … but if only my bill weren't rotting away …"

"You've got to let that go. Say, what if we went over to Tok's?"

"Tok despises me. Because I can't just brashly toss my family aside like he has."

"All right then, let's go to Craback's."

In the time since that concert, I had become friends with the great musician, so I decided to take Rapp over to his house. Compared with Tok, Craback lived in far greater luxury—which is not to say that he lived extravagantly, nothing like that capitalist Geyl. Just that Craback had a lot of antiques—he had a Turkish-style sofa in a room packed with Tanagra figurines and Persian carpets—and he was always playing with his children beneath his own portrait. Today, however, he was sitting around scowling for some reason, his arms crossed over his chest. Scraps of crumpled paper lay scattered all around his feet. Presumably Rapp had seen Craback on several previous occasions with Tok. But this time, Rapp seemed daunted by the musician's demeanor and simply bowed politely as he silently took a seat in a corner of the room.

"What's wrong, Craback?" I asked the great musician, in lieu of a greeting.

"I'm at my wit's end with these blundering critics! They claim that my lyric poems don't hold a candle to Tok's."

"But you're a musician..."

"If that were all, I might be able to take it. But he went on to say that, compared to Rok, I don't deserve to call myself a musician!"

Rok was indeed another musician to whom Craback was often likened. Though, unfortunately I'd never had the chance to speak to him since he wasn't a member of the Übermensch Club. I'd only ever seen photos of him, his upturned bill contributing to the impression that he might be a handful.

"Rok is indeed a genius. But his music lacks the modern passion that yours brims with."

"Do you really think so?"

"I absolutely do."

Just then, Craback stood up, grabbed one of the Tanagra figurines, and flung it on the floor. Rapp appeared rather shaken, emitting some kind of noise as he tried to flee. But Craback made a small gesture toward the two of us, as if to reassure us, and then he said icily:

"That's because you have the ears of a layperson—you don't get it. I'm afraid of Rok..."

"You? Come on, stop playing humble!"

"Who's playing humble? To begin with, if I were going to put on airs, I'd be doing it for the critics, not for you two. I'm—or should I say Craback is—a genius. But that's not why I'm afraid of Rok."

"Well, why are you afraid of him?"

"It's something intangible... perhaps, if I had to say, it's the star that Rok was born under."

"I haven't the slightest clue what you're talking about."

"Then let me put it this way. I have no influence on Rok. But, somehow or other, Rok has come to influence me."

"That's just your receptive nature—"

"Oh, listen here now. It's not a matter of being receptive. Rok is always content to do work that he alone can do. But me, I get frustrated. From Rok's perspective, it might only seem to be the difference of a single stride. But for me, it sets us miles apart."

"But, sir," Rapp ventured, "your Eroica Symphony—"

Craback narrowed his already small eyes and glared at Rapp with seeming irritation.

"Shut up! Your kind just don't get it. I know Rok. I know him better than the dogs who throw themselves at his feet."

"Hey, calm down!"

"If only I could... All I ever think about is... that something or other, who knows what … has set Rok before me in order to mock me, poor old Craback. Magg the philosopher knows all about this sort of thing. Even though he spends all his time reading dusty old books under that colored glass lantern."

"What do you mean?"

"Have a look at the book Magg just wrote, *Words of a Fool*.

Craback handed me a book—or perhaps it would be more apt to say he threw it at me.

"Well, that'll be all for today," he declared gruffly, folding his arms again.

I decided to go back out on the street with the despondent Rapp. It was as bustling as ever with the pedestrians and the array of shops shaded by beech trees. Not having much to say, we walked along in silence—when who should we happen to run into but the long-haired poet Tok. Upon seeing us, he pulled a handkerchief from his stomach pouch and wiped his brow repeatedly.

"Hey there, haven't seen you for a while," Tok said. "I thought I'd go visit Craback today for a change …"

Wary of an argument arising between these artistic types, I informed Tok in so many words that Craback was not in the best of moods.

"I see. Then perhaps I won't. Craback does suffer from neurasthenia, doesn't he? … Come to think of it, I haven't been sleeping so well myself these past few weeks and it's taking a toll."

"Well, then, why not take a walk with us?"

"No, not today, thanks."

Suddenly Tok cried out, grabbing my arm: "Yikes!"

He seemed to have broken out in a cold sweat from head to toe.

"What is it?" "What's the matter?" Rapp and I exclaimed in unison.

"Why, just now, I thought I saw a green monkey sticking its head out the window of that car."

Growing somewhat concerned, I suggested that perhaps he should have a consultation with Dr. Chac. However, Tok balked at this; he wasn't having it. What's more, he regarded my face and Rapp's, comparing us rather dubiously, and then spat out:

"I'm no anarchist, you know! And I urge you never to forget it ... Good day, then. And please forgive me about Chac."

Rapp and I stood there stupefied, as we watched Tok's retreating figure. We—actually, I shouldn't say "we." Without my noticing, Rapp was now standing in the middle of the street: his feet were splayed wide, he was bent over, and he was peering between his legs at the steady stream of traffic and passersby. As I pulled Rapp upright, I wondered with astonishment if this Kappa too had gone mad.

"That isn't funny. What are you doing?"

Rapp simply rubbed his eyes, responding with unexpected composure:

"Well, since I'd been feeling so depressed, I thought I'd try looking at the world upside down. But turns out, it's exactly the same."

Chapter 11

HERE ARE SEVERAL APHORISMS from *Words of a Fool*, written by Magg the philosopher.

A fool believes that everyone other than himself is a fool.

*

It may be that the reason we love nature is because it expresses neither jealousy nor hatred toward us.

*

The wisest way to live is to scorn the customs of one's age while still abiding by them.

*

We are proudest of what we don't have.

*

No one objects to destroying idols. At the same time, no one objects to becoming an idol themselves. Yet, he who can rest easily on a pedestal is blessed by the gods to the highest degree—and is either a fool, a scoundrel, or a hero. [*These lines bore the traces of Craback's scratch marks.*]

*

It may be that thought—at least, that which is necessary for our lives—reached its apex 3,000 years ago. Since then, we have merely been adding kindling to the fire.

*

We are characterized by our tendency to transcend our own consciousness

*

If happiness goes hand in hand with pain, and peace accompanies boredom … ?

*

It is more difficult to defend oneself than it is to defend others. If anyone doubts this, they merely have to observe a lawyer.

*

Pride, lust, doubt—for three thousand years, all our sins have stemmed from these three things. As well as all our virtues.

Limiting one's material desires does not always bring us peace. In order to have peace, we must also limit our spiritual desires. [*These lines, too, bore Craback's scratch marks.*]

*

We are more unhappy than humans. Humans are not as evolved as Kappas. [*When I read this, I instinctively chuckled to myself.*]

*

To attempt something is to be able to do it; to be able to do something is to attempt to do it. Ultimately we are unable to escape this vicious circle. In other words, we begin and end in absurdity.

*

After Baudelaire went mad, he expressed his life philosophy in one word—*cunt*. However, it's not necessarily the case that he himself said this. If anything, it was because he relied entirely on his poetic genius to support himself that he forgot a much more important word: *stomach*. [*Here, again, was evidence of Craback's scratchings.*]

*

If reason were truly the beginning and end of all things, we would have to deny our own existence.

That Voltaire happily spent his whole life worshiping reason demonstrates that humans are not as evolved as Kappas.

Chapter 12

IT HAPPENED ONE relatively cold afternoon. I had grown bored with *Words of a Fool*, so I was setting out to see Magg the philosopher, when who should I happen to see but that Kappa who had stolen my fountain pen! He was wiry as a mosquito, leaning idly against a wall on a desolate street corner. *I've got him*, I thought, hailing a tough-looking police officer who happened to be passing by just then.

"Sir, please question this Kappa. About one month ago, he stole my fountain pen."

The officer raised the baton in his right hand (in Kappa Land, policemen carry a rod made from swamp cypress instead of a sword) and called out to the Kappa in question, "Hey, you there!" I had expected the Kappa to run away. But, on the contrary, he approached the officer with calm composure. Not only that, with arms still crossed, he stared at both me and the patrolman rather defiantly, scrutinizing our faces. Yet the officer showed no trace of anger. Instead, he simply reached into his stomach pouch, took out a notebook, and began to question the Kappa.

"Your name?"

"Gruk."

"Occupation?"

"Up until two or three days ago, I was a postman."

"Very well. So then, this person alleges that you stole his fountain pen."

"Yes, I stole it a month or so ago."

"For what purpose?"

"I thought it would make a good plaything for my child."

"And did it?" For the first time, the officer gave the Kappa a sharp look.

"My child died a week ago."

"Do you have a death certificate?"

The skinny Kappa produced a piece of paper from his stomach pouch. The officer looked it over, then broke into a sudden knowing smile and patted him on the shoulder.

"Very well. Many thanks for your trouble."

I stared at the policeman, completely dumbfounded. Meanwhile, the skinny Kappa turned and walked away from us, muttering something under his breath. Once I managed to collect myself, I inquired of the officer:

"Why didn't you arrest him?"

"The Kappa had not committed a crime."

"But he stole my fountain pen . . ."

"It was to be a toy for his child. But now that child has died. If you have any questions, please refer to Section Twelve-Eighty-Five of the Criminal Code."

With this, the patrolman quickly headed off elsewhere. There was nothing more I could do, so I rushed to Magg's house, repeating to myself "Section Twelve-Eighty-Five, Section Twelve-Eighty-Five." Magg the philosopher enjoys playing host. Indeed, on that day, Judge Pepp, Dr. Chac, and Geyl the glass company president were all gathered in his dimly lit parlor, the smoke from their tobacco drifting up toward the iridescent stained-glass lantern. It was most serendipitous that Judge Pepp was there. As soon as I took a seat, I began questioning him about Section Twelve-Eighty-Five of the Criminal Code, rather than looking it up myself.

"Pepp, my friend, forgive me for asking, but does this country not punish its criminals?"

Pepp took a leisurely drag off his gold-tipped cigarette before responding with deep ennui:

"We absolutely do. We even carry out the death penalty."

"And yet, a month or so ago ..."

And here I launched into the particulars of the event, before asking about Section Twelve-Eighty-Five.

"Hmm, well, here's what it says: 'Even when a crime has been committed, if the circumstances under which said crime was committed are no longer in effect, then the criminal in question cannot be punished.' In other words, in your case, that Kappa used to be a parent, but since he is no longer a parent, the crime is automatically rendered null and void."

"That's simply absurd," I replied.

"Don't kid yourself. It's even more absurd to treat a

Kappa who used to be a parent the same way as a Kappa who currently is one. But Japanese law treats them as the same, doesn't it? We find that simply hilarious, *fu-fu-fu-fu-fu*," Pepp said, enunciating an extended snicker. His expression was lackadaisical as he flicked aside his cigarette.

At that point Chac cut in—though he had no connection to the law.

"Do you have the death penalty in Japan?" he asked as he adjusted his pince-nez.

"Absolutely. We hang them." I had sensed a somewhat icy hostility from Pepp, so I took the opportunity to make a sarcastic remark. "I assume the death penalty in this country must be more civilized than in Japan?"

"Of course it's more civilized," Pepp said, unperturbed. "Here we do not hang criminals. On rare occasions, we use electricity. But generally we don't. We simply name the crime and call them out on it."

"And that's enough to make a Kappa die?"

"Absolutely. We Kappas have much more sensitive nervous systems than you do."

"And that doesn't just apply to the death penalty. The same method can be used for murder," Geyl said, smiling amiably, his face bathed in purple light from the colored lantern. "Recently, a socialist said to me, 'You're a thief, you bastard,' and that was enough to bring on a heart attack."

"It happens surprisingly often. I knew a lawyer who died that way."

I looked around to see which Kappa had said this—it was Magg the philosopher. He wore his usual wry smile, and he spoke without looking at anyone in particular.

"Somebody had called him a frog—in this country, as you know, to call a Kappa a frog is basically equivalent to calling him a fiendish beast … Anyway, the lawyer was tormented by this, wondering day in and day out, *Am I a frog? Am I not a frog?* And soon enough, he up and died.

"That sounds like it was suicide."

"But the Kappa who called him a frog said he intended to kill him. So then, would you still call that suicide …?"

Just as Magg said this, from beyond the walls a sound suddenly ricocheted through the air—the piercing blast of a pistol fired from what had to be the poet Tok's house.

Chapter 13

WE DASHED OVER to Tok's house immediately. There, we found him lying face up in a potted alpine plant, blood spilling from the plate atop his head, right hand gripping a pistol. By his side, a female Kappa had her head buried in his chest and was wailing at the top of her lungs.

"What happened?" I asked, putting my arms around her to help her up (though to be honest, I don't very much like touching a Kappa's slimy skin with my hands).

"I don't know! I thought he was just in here writing something, when all of a sudden he shot himself in the head. Ahh, what am I going to do now? *qur-r-r-r-r, qur-r-r-r-r.*" (That's the sound they make when crying).

"That Tok ... he really was quite the selfish one," said Geyl the glass company president, shaking his head sadly. But Judge Pepp simply lit a gold-tipped cigarette and said nothing.

"It's no use. Tok always did have stomach troubles, which meant he was susceptible to depression," Chac declared to the five of us (well, it was one human and four

Kappas). Up until now he had been on his hands and knees, examining Tok's wound in true doctor fashion.

"His wife said he was writing something," murmured Magg, the philosopher, as though in Tok's defense. As he picked up the piece of paper that lay on the desk, we all craned our necks over his wide shoulders (well, everyone except me) to see what it said.

> *Come, let us go*
> *To the valley that cuts through this fleeting world*
> *Where the rocky crags are steep, and over it the mountain*
> *   stream runs pure*
> *Where the herbs are fragrant.*

"Wait a minute, this is plagiarized from Goethe's *Mignon's Song*," Magg said as he turned around to look at us, a wry smile on his face. "Tok must have been quite burnt out on writing poetry, hence his suicide."

Just then, a car drove up to the house, bearing Craback the musician. He lingered a while in the doorway as he surveyed the scene. But when he walked over to us, he began shouting at Magg, almost hectoring him:

"Is that Tok's last will and testament?"

"No, it's the final poem he wrote."

"Poem?"

Magg remained unperturbed as he handed the manuscript over to Craback, who began to read it with a fierce concentration, hair standing wildly on end, not letting his eyes stray from the page for an instant. He only barely responded to Magg's questions.

"So, what do you think of Tok's death?"

"*Come, let us go … I myself don't know when I will die … To the valley that cuts through this fleeting world …*"

"But weren't you one of Tok's closest friends?"

"Closest friend? Tok was always alone … *To the valley that cuts through this fleeting world …* but despite his unhappiness … *Where the rocky crags are steep …*"

"Despite his unhappiness?"

"*The mountain stream runs pure …* You all are happy. *Where the rocky crags are steep …*"

I felt quite sorry for the female Kappa, who was still sobbing, so I gently put my arm around her shoulder and led her to a couch in the corner of the room. There was a two- or three-year-old Kappa child who was smiling, not understanding what was going on. Now I began to comfort the Kappa child instead of the female Kappa. And before I knew it, I felt tears fill my eyes. That was the first and last time I ever cried in Kappa Land.

"I do feel quite sorry for the family who ended up with this selfish Kappa," said Geyl the capitalist.

"Right, he never thought about what would happen after his death," answered Judge Pepp as he lit yet another cigarette.

Just then, we were startled by the voice of Craback the musician, who was yelling at no one in particular while still gripping the sheet of poetry.

"Aha, I've got it! I can make a brilliant requiem out of this!"

His small eyes glittering, Craback briefly grasped Magg's hands, before suddenly dashing off toward the doorway. Of course, by this time, a crowd of neighbors had gathered around the entrance to Tok's home, and were peering inside with curious expressions. But Craback simply pushed and shoved his way through the crowd, then leapt lightly into the car. The engine gave a loud roar, and in an instant he was gone.

"Hey now, you can't all come poking your heads in like this," said Judge Pepp, playing policeman as he pushed the Kappas out, and then shut Tok's door.

Perhaps it was for that reason that the room suddenly became strangely quiet. And within this quiet—amid the scent of alpine flowers mixed with the smell of Tok's blood—we conferred about how to deal with the aftermath. Only Magg the philosopher remained standing, gazing at Tok's dead body. He seemed to be pondering something. I tapped him on the shoulder.

"What are you thinking about?" I asked him.

"The life of a Kappa."

"What about the life of a Kappa?"

"Whatever we may say, in order to live out our Kappa lives to the fullest . . ."

Then he added in a small voice, as though slightly embarrassed, "In any case, we must believe in the power of something or someone greater than us Kappas."

Chapter 14

WHAT MAGG SAID made me think about religion. I'm a materialist, so of course I've never given any serious thought to the subject. However, Tok's death had had a certain effect on me, and it led me to wonder: just what was Kappa religion anyway? I promptly posed this question to Rapp the student.

"Well, we practice Christianity, Buddhism, Islam, Zoroastrianism, and so on, though Nowism is probably what has the most influence. We also call it Lifeism." ("Lifeism" is really not an accurate equivalent. The original Kappa word is *Quemoocha*. The *cha* suffix means the same as the English *ism* while *quemoo* comes from the base form of *quemal*, which, much more than simply "life," means "eating, drinking, and copulating.")

"So, you have churches and temples and the like here too?" I asked.

"Are you kidding? The Great Temple of Nowism is the grandest building in Kappa Land. Say, why don't we go for a visit?"

So one warm, hazy afternoon, Rapp proudly took me to the Great Temple. Just as promised, it was ten times the size of the Holy Resurrection Cathedral in Tokyo. Not only that, the edifice incorporated every architectural style into its construction. As I stood before it, gazing at its tall stupas and domes, an eerie feeling came over me: they looked like so many tentacles stretching up toward the heavens. The two of us stood by the entrance (we must have seemed miniscule, seen in perspective with such a doorway!), looking up at this building that was more like a chimerical monster than a peerlessly designed sanctuary.

The interior of the Great Temple was similarly vast. There were numerous visitors milling around inside, amid the Corinthian columns. They too seemed incredibly small in comparison. Before long, we encountered a Kappa, his back bent with age. Rapp bowed slightly and said politely: "Glad to see you're looking fit as a fiddle, Elder!"

The Kappa bowed in return and responded, just as politely:

"Is that you, Rapp? You too, as ever …" (As he said these words, though, he seemed to take notice of Rapp's rotting bill, which gave him pause.) "… Ah, well, you seem healthy enough, anyway. So, what brings you here today?"

"I'm accompanying this gentleman here. You may already have heard of him …" Rapp then proceeded to speak effusively about me. I seemed to be his excuse for why he had hardly been coming by the temple. "And that being the case, would you be so kind as to give him a tour?"

The Elder smiled magnanimously as he greeted me and then, without a word, pointed at the front altar.

"I'm afraid I can't be of much help in that regard. Our adherents worship what we call the 'Tree of Life' at the front altar there. As you can see, the Tree of Life bears golden fruit and green fruit. The golden fruit is called 'The Fruit of Virtue' and the green fruit is called 'The Fruit of Evil' ..."

I found his explanations quite boring. This was because, despite the Elder's graciousness, his turns of phrase reminded me of dated parables. Of course I feigned rapt attention. But, every so often, I made a point of stealing a glance around the interior of the Great Temple.

The features and furnishings—the Corinthian columns, the vaulted Gothic ceilings, the Moorish checkered floor, the pseudo-Secession prayer kneelers—created a harmony replete with a strange and savage beauty. But it was the marble busts set into niches along the sides of the hall that most captured my attention. I had a sense that I recognized these likenesses—and no wonder. Once the stooped Kappa finished his explanation about the Tree of Life, he then walked Rapp and me over to one of the niches on the right, where he offered details about the bust enshrined there.

"Here is one of our saints, Strindberg, who rebelled against everything. It is said that, after much struggle and torment, this saint was saved by the philosophy of Swedenborg. But, in fact, he was not saved. Like us, this saint believed in Lifeism—or rather, he had no choice but to believe in it. Have a gander at the book that this saint left behind for us called *Legends*. He confessed to having attempted to kill himself."

I found this a bit depressing, and glanced over at the next niche. Enshrined there was the bust of a stout, mustachioed German.

"Here is Nietzsche, the poet of Zarathustra. This saint sought salvation from the Übermensch, which he conceived of himself. But, in the end, he was not saved—he lost his mind. Though it may be that, had he not lost his mind, he wouldn't be counted among our saints …"

The Elder was silent for a moment, and then he guided us in front of the third niche.

"The third one is Tolstoy. He was the most ascetic of the saints. (This was because, having been born an aristocrat, he hated to reveal his suffering to the ever-curious peasants.) This saint strived to believe in the effectively unbelievable Christ. Oh, he even publicly declared his beliefs. However, in his later years he came to view those beliefs as unbearable and tragic lies. Famously, Tolstoy sometimes feared the roofbeams in his own study. But since he numbers among the saints, naturally he didn't die by suicide."

The bust in the fourth niche was one of our own Japanese. I could not help feeling a pang of homesickness when I saw his face.

"Here is Kunikida Doppo. A poet who truly understood the sentiments of the laborer who throws himself in front of an oncoming train. But obviously, being Japanese, you need no further explanation on this topic. Have a look at the fifth niche …"

"Isn't that Wagner?"

"It is. The revolutionary who was friends with the king.

In his later years Saint Wagner even said grace before meals. But of course, more than being a Christian, he was, first and foremost, a believer in Lifeism. If you read his letters, it's clear that before his death he was consumed with the suffering of this world."

By this time we were already standing before the sixth niche.

"Here is Strindberg's friend. The French businessman turned painter who traded his wife, the mother of his many children, for a Tahitian girl of thirteen. This saint had the blood of a sailor coursing through his veins. But look closely at his lips. There's a trace of arsenic on them. Now, in the seventh niche … Oh, you must be getting tired. All right, then, come on over here, if you will."

I was in fact quite tired, so Rapp and I followed the Elder along a corridor that smelled distinctly of incense, and then entered a room. In one corner, there was a black statue of Venus. At her feet was an offering, a cluster of crimson glory vine. I found this a bit unexpected, having imagined that a monk's quarters would be unadorned. The Elder, seeing the look on my face and guessing my feelings, explained, half apologetically, "Please don't forget that our religion is Lifeism," and then he offered us a seat. "Our god, the Tree of Life, teaches us to 'live avidly.' — Rapp, have you shown this gentleman our scriptures?"

"No … To be honest, I hardly know them myself," Rapp replied candidly as he scratched the plate on his head.

The Elder smiled, as gently as before, and went on talking.

"In that case, it's unlikely you would understand. Our

god created this world in the span of a day. (The Tree of Life may be a tree, but there's nothing it can't do.) Not only that, it created the female Kappa. Eventually the female Kapp grew so bored that she asked for a male Kappa. Our god felt her sorrow and took pity, and from her brain created a male Kappa. Our god gave these two Kappas his benediction, 'Eat, copulate, and live avidly' ..."

While the Elder was speaking, I thought about Tok the poet. Unfortunately, Tok had been an atheist like me. Not being a Kappa, I couldn't be blamed for being ignorant about Lifeism. But Tok, having been born in Kappa Land, should have been familiar with the Tree of Life. I pitied Tok's end, his lack of awareness of these teachings, and I interrupted the Elder to mention him.

"Ah, yes, that poor poet." The Elder listened to what I had to say, and then let out a deep sigh. "Our fate is determined by three factors alone: faith, circumstance, and chance. (Though you all, I'm sure, would count genetics among these as well.) Unfortunately Tok lacked faith."

"Tok must have envied you," I said. "Oh, I envy you too. Rapp, well ... he's still young ..."

"If only my bill were in better shape, I might be more happy-go-lucky."

The Elder let out another deep sigh at these remarks. Moved to tears, he kept his gaze fixed on the black Venus.

"The truth is—and this is a secret, so please don't tell a soul—the truth is I cannot bring myself to believe in our god. And someday my prayers ..."

It happened just as he said this. Suddenly the door flew open and a large female Kappa swiftly leapt at the Elder.

Naturally Rapp and I tried to catch hold of her. But the female had wrestled the Elder to the floor in the blink of an eye.

"This old coot! He's gone and stolen more money from my wallet for his booze—haven't you?!"

After about ten minutes, Rapp and I fled the scene as inconspicuously as we could, leaving the elderly couple behind as we exited the Great Temple.

After walking along in silence for a while, Rapp said to me, "Considering all that, it's no wonder the Elder doesn't believe in the Tree of Life."

Instead of responding, I instinctively turned back to look at the Great Temple. Its stupas and domes were still stretching up into the leaden, overcast sky like so many tentacles. Giving off all the eeriness of a mirage you might see in the desert sky ...

Chapter 15

ABOUT A WEEK or so after that, I heard an interesting story from Chac: apparently Tok's house was haunted. By then, his girlfriend had gone off somewhere, and our friend the poet's house had been converted into a photographer's studio. According to Chac, every time a photograph was taken in this studio, a hazy but still definitive image of Tok would appear behind the subject in the photo. Of course, being a materialist, Chac didn't believe in life beyond death. When he recounted this story, he smiled wryly, adding, "So it seems souls have a material basis after all." I, like Chac, do not believe in ghosts. But I did feel an affection for Tok, so, without any delay, I rushed over to the bookstore and purchased every newspaper and magazine I could find that included photographs of Tok's ghost, as well as any related articles. And indeed, as I examined the photographs, there he was — a hazy but decidedly Tok-like figure, appearing somewhere or other behind the Kappas in every portrait. But what shocked me more than seeing images of Tok's ghost were the articles about it—in particular, a report from the Society for the Study of Psychical Phenomena. I have translated this report quite faithfully, and I will give a brief outline of it below. Please note, however, that the words in brackets are my own annotations—

"Report Concerning the Ghost of the Poet Tok" (*Journal of the Society for the Study of Psychical Phenomena*, Vol. 8274)

We, the Society for the Study of Psychical Phenomena, have convened a special meeting at No 251 —— Street, the former residence of Mr. Tok and currently used as a studio by the photographer —— to investigate the late poet's recent suicide. [*I have excised the actual names here.*]

We, the seventeen members of the Society for the Study of Psychical Phenomena, along with the president of the society, Mr. Pek, and accompanied by our most trusted medium Madame Hopp, gathered in one of the rooms of said studio at 10:30 a.m. on September 17. When Madame Hopp entered the studio in question, she immediately sensed a ghostly presence in the room and began having full-body convulsions, even going so far as to vomit several times. According to madame, due to the poet Tok's intense love of tobacco, that ghostly air contained nicotine.

We members, along with Madame Hopp, sat at a round table in silence. After three minutes and twenty-five seconds, she fell abruptly into a somnambulistic trance as her body was seemingly taken possession of by the poet Tok. We members took turns, going in order by age, in asking the poet Tok—whose spirit was possessing Madame Hopp's body—the following questions:

Q: For what reason do you appear now as a ghost?

A: Because I wish to know what reputation I have gained since my death..

Q: So you—or your spirit—still seek fame beyond death?

A: I, at least, find it difficult to resist. However, there is one Japanese poet I happened to meet who scorns the idea of posthumous fame.

Q: And do you know that poet's name?

A: Unfortunately, I have forgotten it. I do, however, remember a seventeen-syllable poem of his that he was rather fond of.

Q: And what is that poem?

A: "The quiet pond. A frog leaps in. The sound of the water."

Q: And you claim that's a fine poem?

A: Oh no, it is definitely a bad poem. But if the word "Kappa" were substituted for "frog," it would be absolutely brilliant.

Q: And why do you say that?

A: Because we Kappas are always keen to seek ourselves in every work of art.

At this point, Mr. Pek, the president of the society, reminded our seventeen members that this was a special meeting convened by the Society for the Study of Psychical Phenomena—not an art appreciation group.

Q: What is life like as a ghost?

A: No different from yours.

Q: And do you regret the fact of your own suicide?

A: Not in the slightest. And besides, if I ever tire of

being a ghost, I can always pick up a pistol and commit myself back to life.

Q: And is that an easy thing, committing oneself back to life?

[*Tok's ghost responded to this question with another question. Those who know Tok will recognize this as a very typical exchange with him.*]

A: Is it an easy thing to commit suicide?

Q: Don't ghosts live forever?

A: You shouldn't believe just any old thing you hear about us. Don't forget that, luckily, there are Christians, Buddhists, Muslims, Zoroastrians, and many other religious adherents among us.

Q: And what do you believe?

A: I have always been a skeptic.

Q: Then shouldn't you doubt the existence of ghosts?

A: I am unable to believe in them to the degree that you all do.

Q: How many friends do you have?

A: My friends cross all time and place, numbering no less than three hundred. To name just a few of the more well-known ones, Kleist, Mainländer, Weininger ...

Q: Did all of your friends commit suicide?

A: Not necessarily. For example, I consider Montaigne, who was a defender of suicide, one of my esteemed friends. On the other hand, I do not associate with the likes of the great pessimist Schopenhauer, who incidentally did not commit suicide.

Q: Is Schopenahuer still in good health?

A: At present, he has just established something called Spiritual Pessimism, and is debating the arguments for and against committing oneself back to life. However, having recently learned that cholera is spread through bacteria, he seems much more at ease.

The members of the society then took turns asking about the ghosts of Napoleon, Confucius, Dostoevsky, Darwin, Cleopatra, the Buddha, Demosthenes, Dante, and Sen no Rikyu. But unfortunately Tok did not respond to these questions in detail—instead he asked about various items of gossip related to himself.

Q: How has my reputation been since my death?

A: One critic has taken to calling you a "minor poet."

Q: He must be the one who holds a grudge against me because I did not present him with a copy of my poetry collection. By the way, have my collected works been published yet?

A: Your collected works have been published, but sales weren't brisk.

Q: I'm sure that everyone will buy my collected works in three hundred years—that is, once the copyright has expired. How is the lady Kappa who used to live with me?

A: She has become the wife of the bookseller Rak.

Q: Unfortunately she must still not be aware that Rak has a glass eye. How is my child?

A: I have heard that he has been taken in by the state orphanage.

Tok was silent for a moment, and then began to ask questions anew.

Q: How is my house?

A: It has been converted into the studio of a certain photographer.

Q: And what has become of my desk?

A: We have no idea.

Q: There is a cherished stack of letters in the drawer of my desk—but happily, you all are too busy to bother with those. And now, our spirit world is slowly descending into twilight. I should take my leave of you gentlemen. Farewell, everyone. Farewell, my good people.

With these last words, Madame Hopp abruptly regained consciousness. We, the seventeen members of the society, do solemnly swear before G-d that this dialogue is true to the best of our knowledge. (As for the compensation paid to our trusted medium, Madame Hopp, it's calculated according to the daily wage that she received in her former career as an actress.)

Chapter 16

AFTER READING THESE ARTICLES, I gradually became more depressed about being in Kappa Land. Somehow or other, I felt a desire to return home to our country of humans. But no matter how much I searched, I couldn't find the hole down which I had fallen. At some point, Bagg the fisherman told me about an old Kappa who apparently lived a quiet life on the outskirts of town, reading books and playing the flute. I wondered whether he might know a way out of this country. So I immediately decided to go looking for him. But when I arrived at that little house, instead of an old Kappa I found a young one living there, barely twelve or thirteen, with an unhardened head plate, leisurely playing his flute. Naturally I assumed I must be at the wrong house. But, just in case, I asked the Kappa his name, and he turned out to be the very same elderly Kappa that Bagg had informed me about.

"But you look like a child . . ."

"My dear lad, don't you know the story? As fate would have it, I emerged from my mother's belly with a head of gray hair! From then on I grew progressively younger, eventually becoming the child you see before you now. But assuming I was about sixty when I was born, if you add it all up, I must be about a hundred and fifteen or sixteen by now."

I looked around the room. It may have been my imagination, but I sensed a clear strain of happiness emanating from the modest chairs and table there.

"You do appear to live more happily than other Kappas."

"Say now, that may well be. I was a geezer when I was young, and became a youngster when I got old. Therefore, my desires did not recede as they do for the aged, nor do I indulge in sensual pleasures like most young Kappas. In any case, even if my life hasn't been happy, it's certainly been peaceful."

"It certainly seems that way, from everything you've said."

"But that alone wouldn't make for a peaceful life! I've had good health and enough wealth to never go hungry my whole life. Still, I believe however that my greatest happiness was being born an old man."

I spoke to this Kappa for a while about such things as Tok's suicide and about Geyl who had to see a doctor every day. However, for some reason the old Kappa didn't appear very much interested in what I was saying.

"You don't seem to have quite the same attachment to life as other Kappas, do you?"

The old Kappa looked me in the eye as he calmly replied:

"Like anyone else, I left my mother's womb only after

being asked by my father whether or not I wanted to be born."

"But I tumbled into this country entirely by chance. And now, if you would be so kind as to tell me how I can get out of this place?"

"There's only one way out of here."

"And what is that?"

"The same way you came in, my dear lad."

For some reason, his answer made my hair stand on end. "But I cannot find that way in," I said.

The old Kappa fixed his youthful eyes on me. Then, at last, he got up and walked over to a corner of the room where he pulled on a cord that hung down from the ceiling. When he did so, a skylight that I had not noticed before opened. On the other side of that round skylight, a clear blue cloudless sky extended beyond the branches of pine and cypress. And there, resembling a giant arrowhead, rose the peak of Mount Yari. I leapt with joy, truly like a child who had seen an airplane for the first time.

"See now, here's how you can get out of here," the old Kappa said as he pointed at the cord—or I looked at what I'd thought was a cord, but had now, in fact, become a rope ladder.

"Well then, I'll go out through there," I said.

"But let me tell you something before you go. Make sure you'll have no regrets about leaving."

"I'll be fine," I replied at once, as I scrambled up the rope ladder: "I have no regrets." And then I was looking down at the plate on the old Kappa's head far below.

Chapter 17

FOR SOME TIME after I came back from Kappa Land,
I couldn't stand the smell of human skin—for compared
to us humans, Kappas are actually quite clean creatures.
Not only that, having become accustomed to seeing only
Kappas now I found the sight of human faces quite creepy.
It may strike the reader as odd, but this thing we call a
nose—never mind the eyes or the mouth—awakened in
me the utmost fear and revulsion. Naturally I contrived
to have as little contact with other people as possible. But
gradually I seemed to readjust to being around us humans, and within six months or so I was going out again
with my usual regularity. The only problem was that from
time to time, a word from the Kappa language would slip
out while I was talking.

"Will you be at home tomorrow?"

"*Qua.*"

"Come again?"

"I mean yes, I'll be at home."

And the conversation would proceed like that.

But just about a year after I had come back from Kappa Land, I experienced a certain business failing and … [*When the patient said this, Dr. S admonished him to leave off with that story. According to Dr. S, whenever he would begin to talk about this particular incident, he would become so violent that even the nurses were unable to restrain him.*]

Never mind about that story, then. Anyhow, because of said business failure, I was struck with a desire to return to Kappa Land. That's right—I don't mean "go for a visit." I felt the urge to return there. By then, Kappa Land felt like home to me.

I slipped out of my house quietly and tried to board the Chuo Line train. But unfortunately I was apprehended by a police officer there, and committed to this hospital. Even after I arrived here, I continued to think about Kappa Land for quite some time—what was Dr. Chac up to? Perhaps Magg the philosopher was still sitting beneath his iridescent stained-glass lantern, pondering something. And what about my good friend Rapp, the student with the rotting bill—? I was absorbed in such recollections one cloudy afternoon, much like this one, when I spontaneously let out a cry. Without my noticing, the Kappa fisherman Bagg had somehow wandered in and was now standing right before me, bowing his head repeatedly. After I had regained my composure—in truth I don't remember whether I laughed or cried—but, in any case, what I do know for certain is how good it felt to be speaking the Kappa language again after such a long time.

"Hey, Bagg, what are you doing here?"

"Well, I heard you were sick and so I came to see you."

"How did you know that?"

"I heard it on the news," Bagg said, a triumphant grin on his face.

"Even so, it must have been difficult for you to get here."

"Whatever are you talking about? No trouble at all! The rivers and canals of Tokyo are like roads to us Kappas."

It occurred to me then, rather belatedly, that Kappas were amphibious creatures, like frogs.

"But there aren't many rivers around here."

"I got here by climbing up through the iron water pipes, and opening the fire hydrants a little ..."

"Opening the fire hydrants?"

"Did you forget, sir? That there are mechanics among us Kappas too?"

And from then on, every two or three days, one Kappa or another would come to call on me. My diagnosis, according to Dr. S, was something called dementia praecox. However, Dr. Chac said—and no doubt this will come off as quite offensive to you, as well—that it is not I who has dementia praecox, but Dr. S and you yourself who suffer from it. Even Dr. Chac made it all the way here, so it was a matter of course that Rapp the student and Magg the philosopher came to see me as well. However, only Bagg the fisherman came to visit during the day. Otherwise, two or three of them would visit together at night—and always on nights when the moon was out. Why, just last night I sat in the moonlight talking with Geyl the glass company president and Magg the philosopher. Craback the musician even played me a tune on his violin. Look—see that bouquet of black lilies on the desk over there? That's a gift Craback brought me ...

(I turned around to look behind me. But, of course, there was no bouquet of flowers on the desk.)

And this book, the philosopher Magg kindly brought it for me. Here, read the first poem. Oh—of course, you don't understand the Kappa language. Here, I'll read it for you. This is one of the volumes from Tok's collected works that was published recently—

[*Here he opened an old telephone book and read aloud the following poem:*]

> —*Among the palm flowers and the bamboo*
> *The Buddha is fast asleep.*
>
> *Christ, it seems, is already dead*
> *Along with the withered fig tree by the roadside.*
>
> *But we must rest*
> *Even if only against the backdrop of a stage.*
>
> *(and if we peered behind the backdrop, we would only*
> *find a patchwork canvas on the other side!)*—

But I am not as pessimistic as this poet—as long as the Kappas come and visit me every once in a while. Ah, I almost forgot! You remember my friend, Judge Pepp, don't you? After that Kappa lost his job, he went completely mad. I hear he's now at a mental hospital in Kappa Land. If Dr. S allows it, I'd like to go and pay him a visit ...